My Untimely Death

Subito Press is a nonprofit literary publisher based in the Creative Writing Program of the Department of English at the University of Colorado at Boulder. We look for innovative fiction and poetry that at once reflects and informs the contemporary human condition, and we promote new literary voices as well as work from previously published writers. Subito Press encourages and supports work that challenges already-accepted literary modes and devices.

2007 Competition Winners

Fiction: Adam Peterson, *My Untimely Death*
Poetry: Kristin Abraham, *Little Red Riding Hood Missed the Bus*

Adam Peterson

My Untimely Death

Subito Press / Boulder, Colorado / 2008

Subito Press
Boulder, Colorado
www.subitopress.org

Library of Congress Cataloging in Publication Data
available upon request

ISBN 978-0-9801098-1-8

Generous funding for this publication has been
provided by the Creative Writing Program in the
Department of English at the University of Colorado,
Boulder, as well as the United Government of Graduate
Students (UGGS).

Contents

Acknowledgments

With thanks to the editors, parts of *My Untimely Death* appear in the following publications: *Handsome*, *Ninth Letter*, *La Petite Zine*, *The Cupboard Pamphlet*, *Redactions*, *Redivider*, and *Saltgrass*.

My Untimely Death

One

It is reported that my untimely death was a murder but I know, even as water tickles my bronchi, that it is really only a misunderstanding. The coroner presses his stamp into red ink and punches it down on the report: "MURDER" there in bloody capitals.

I am a breach birth. My writhing legs foreshadow the shock of red hair on my head. The doctor, in the first great confusion of my life, fails to turn me over and slaps my face to make me take my first screaming breath. Instead of inhaling, I exhale a long, dusty breath. One nurse faints. The other crosses her chest and says, It's God's breath.

From that moment I live backward. My parents scream in the mornings when they see me face down in the crib and every morning they wake me. I cry with them. I begin to crawl by doing a crabwalk and by the time we relearn this move as school children, I win the crabwalk race by a full minute. I walk the halls backward, my backpack slung across my chest, one strap off like I see the other kids do. As an adult when I walk the street to work in the morning, everyone else keeps their chin down while mine is high. Their eyes nowhere, mine seek them as they walk behind me, blushing.

A date asks me, Do you eat spaghetti at breakfast and cereal at dinner? Do you smoke a cigarette and then have sex? When this night is over will you say a hello?

I'm not a monster, I answer. I get up from the table, and as I walk away I stare the girl down until her eyes break for the ground.

This talent to see what is behind me leads to love. This is not an accident. I meet a green-eyed woman on the escalator at the mall. I get on backward and she gets on behind me, and the whole ride up our faces are a foot away. Her eyes never leave mine for the ground.

Will you marry me? I say.

Already? she says.

I do things differently, I tell her. She has to go on the

tips of her red shoes to kiss me and I have to bend my knees. When we walk the aisle, newly man and wife, the priest gives me a thumbs up, and it is as if I can see the smiles through the thinning hair on the back of my parents' heads.

She didn't mean to kill me. The night of our honeymoon my wife pours me a bubble bath. I tell her I've never taken a bath, and she kisses me. I walk backward. She walks forward. Our eyes are inches apart until, even so close, steam comes between us. Then she is gone. I am alone in the bathroom. It smells like bees and hospitals. Without looking behind me, I dip a heel in the hot water. It feels like bees and hospitals.

The tub is full of prismatic bubbles, and as I lower myself into the blisteringly hot water I see rainbows broken on the curves. I breathe these rainbows until they are inside my head. Baths are nice, I think. Marriage is nice, I think. When I die I feel very clean.

Two

Spring has come after the longest winter of my life so I lie in the hammock napping while the sun is out and the cicadas are singing and Jon Secada is singing on the small radio I carried out in my left hand while in my right hand I carried a pink lemonade which rests on my sternum wetting a cold circle on my polo, and it is all perfectly spring until everything gets ruined by my untimely death.

My death falls from the sky. At first a dark shadow that might be a cloud—the sun never breaks it. Shade is not spring so, upset, I open my eyes to see a block of what appears to be lead falling toward me. This is not spring, but I close my eyes to it and think how happy I am that a block of lead is not winter either.

This is what it feels like to die: throwing away a letter, building a diorama, hating someone you spend time with, eating your favorite meal on consecutive days, flipping over a blank page in a photo album, the band Bad Company, sleeping next to a dog, buying an expensive pen, seeing a cousin unexpectedly, sampling a taste of your baby's food, aiming a pellet gun, cooking your first meal for one, being late to a job interview.

Mostly it feels like a nursery rhyme I try to remember. It is as if I know this death from somewhere. It was not always a block of lead in the spring. Like all things, I imagined death many ways. It just as easily could have been cobalt, car crash, summer, stab, or more cobalt.

Three

I die a young, untimely death and an anachronistic, untimely death. I find that my untimely death comes to me when nothing else would. Alone, I cough and cough, and when I pull the handkerchief away from my mouth there is one, perfect spot of red blood in the middle. It looks like the Japanese flag, and I hang it above my bed so that I think of sunrises when I wake up. I go to the doctor. He is an old man who practices medicine in his basement. He delivered me in my untimely birth, one month premature, and has guided me through every illness of my childhood and adult life with the nostrum-like reassurance expected of a doctor with a grey mustache.

He pokes my skin with a needle and one, perfect spot of red blood rises to the surface. It looks like Jupiter among the swirls of freckles on my arm. I take a picture with my phone and make it the background so that I think of storms when I want to call my ex-girl-friend. The doctor sucks up the spot of blood with an eyedropper and delicately moves it onto a slide where he examines it with all of the expressions at his dispos-al—hmm; ah, yes; I see; well then; interesting.

You have consumption, he says.

Do people still get consumption? I ask.

Only people like you, he says.

On the way home I buy black clothes and many, many more handkerchiefs. I have read about this, I think. I know what consumptives do. I never go outside and a deathly pallor overtakes my skin. I eat only beef broth and the flesh disappears from my bones. I become ef-fete, sophisticated. I kiss a boy. Sometimes I faint in public. I cough even when I don't have to. There is never any blood.

I return to the doctor. He is surprised that I am still alive, but I tell him I don't think I—or anyone—has consumption anymore. They have another name for it now, I say. Do you think I have tuberculosis? I ask.

Oh, God no, he says. You have a case of the fits.

On the walk home I fall over in the street and begin to shake. I try to foam at the mouth. Everyone steps around me and after six or seven minutes of shaking I become tired so I stand up and go home. I throw away my black clothes, my handkerchiefs. I buy a helmet. I never fall over again. When I again go to the doctor he tells me I have the horrors.

The horrors? I ask.

The horrors, he says.

And this time the diagnosis is correct. I see apparitions that look like people I know, but they are not dead yet. This knowledge causes madness, the fits, consumption. I lay on my bed with my phone open. Above me is the Japanese flag. I cough. I shake at the horrors.

Four

My untimely death is caused by malfunction. Although the last, it is not the first time machines have failed me, and I consider myself lucky to have lived for as long as I have.

At six, a bike I was riding collapsed at the spokes, each one snapping like raw spaghetti until the bike fell to the cement, and I rolled down a hill where my fall broke against the shins of my mother while my red Huffy's bolts unbolted and welds unwelded as the tumbling scraps bore down on us. We might have been killed, but the bolts bolted and welds welded so when it finally stopped bouncing it was a convection oven. My mother picked it up.

My mother rubbed alcohol on my scrapes and made me cookies in our new oven to silence my cries.

On my seventeenth birthday my mother bought me a

car. I knew nothing about my car except that it was a red one and beeped angrily when I opened the doors or lit a clove cigarette. The car never malfunctioned— and it was right about clove cigarettes—but once when I walked through the high school parking lot, a red car suddenly caught fire. One second nothing, the next second fire. Afterward, I took the bus and gave the car to my cousin.

I often have wondered why cars do not catch fire more often, and I tell anyone I sit next to on the bus that we are smart not to be driving cars, especially not red ones. When I get the time to explain more—at dinner parties after having wine or next to a girlfriend in bed—they tell me I am making a statistical error. I tell them cars run on fire.

If I am really drunk at the dinner party or really in love with the girl, I sometimes add that I wouldn't ride in anything run on cancer either. They roll their eyes and kiss me, respectively.

Once, a red pen exploded in my pocket and got all over my money. When I bought a Coke from a machine with the stained bills, the bottle came out with red liquid in it that tasted like birthday cake frosting. I wanted to write a letter to whoever was responsible but did not know what had malfunctioned. The drink was delicious so I broke a Bic in my hands and poured red ink over a pile of singles. I fed them one at a time into the machine. Every bottle that fell was normal Coke.

And then my death at thirty from another imperfection of man's hand, but I cannot remember which one actually killed me. I've been told a train derailed. An elevator cord snapped. A boat capsized. A strong wind from the south caught an old high-rise just so and it fell over like a drunk. I cannot remember which death is mine so I'm writing you this letter.

I won't send it though. This death is delicious.

Five

My untimely death is not a choice.

But I do get a choice. My jailers bring me a list which they claim was long ago written in blood on human skin, but to me it appears ink-jetted in maroon on bonded paper. I recognize the font as Copperplate Gothic.

It's not the original, they claim. Only the warden can see that.

My menu is before me:

1. FIRING SQUAD
2. ~~HANGING~~
3. ELECTRIC CHAIR
4. GAS CHAMBER
5. LETHAL INJECTION
6. STONING
7. DRAWING AND/OR QUARTERING
8. GUILLOTINE

Oh, the jaundiced but pretty guard says, we added one too. With a green ballpoint he writes '9. loNg FaLL' with irregular capitalization. I ask if that's what it looks like on the original blood-and-flesh version. They hit me in the stomach. Only the warden can see that, they say, and only if he has on his special glasses.

Why not hanging? I ask.

Got rid of it after what happened to the fellow in Utah, they say.

What happened to the fellow in Utah? I ask.

They hit me in the stomach and leave. I have the night to think about it. I lick the moss growing on the bars of my cell. It tastes like moldy bread tastes, and I know because I have moldy bread for dinner and my tongue aches from operculum. All night the black coots cry from the marshes. I find a paperclip in the corner of the cell and straighten it. I think little about my death.

At dawn the guards return and ask me to write down the number of my choice in blood so I prick my finger with the straightened paperclip and ask, What flesh have you to write upon? The guards looked confused and pass me a child's composition book through the bars. Other prisoners have written their choice in these pages and the size of the numbers vary, but the color of the blood is always bright like chard. There are many blank pages left. With my bloody finger, I write a 6 of my own lineage. The guards mistake it for a 9 and take me from my cell in a silk blindfold.

It is indeed a long fall, and I have yet to hit bottom though I have chosen, as I have chosen the method, to call it death.

Six

My murder is untimely, but my death takes years until I finally go, an old man with hard-won notions about the morality and taste of you, the new young, that dissipate from my mind as I close my eyes—a late victim.

From a young age I was kept from climbing the poplar trees and brushing my teeth and entering the kitchen. Kept from boyhood, my parents sent me to live in a field of red poppies where the land was flat and nothing could prick my delicate skin. I slept underneath a pink blanket when the pollen made me sleepy. From long poles servants would feed me marshmallows which I ate without utensils. Everything I touched I covered with chalky powder.

When my parents saw me through binoculars I detected the disappointment on their faces about where my hands had been.

At fifteen, the first green of a rose bush sprouted through the ground in the poppy field and at the sight of thorns, generals and spies, and a gardener were called for to cut the stalk down and salt the earth where it had been. I didn't know what was meant by rose, but the word made me quake. I imagined roses blossomed into parents. I imagined parents dropped marshmallows for seeds and the seeds would grow to stop signs and dogs and baseball games. I secretly ate the salted earth in addition to my daily marshmallows.

Then followed my assassination. The envelope awaited me as I woke. When I took it into my hands, my named scrawled in runny blue ink, it gave me a small paper-cut. I was murdered. A drop of blood, like a fire ant, fell from my finger onto an equally red poppy. I was done in. I left my field behind, knowing that should I ever want to come back I could follow my own uncoagulated blood. I carried the envelope in my lacerated hand. Over time it became as red as home, but still I did not open it.

I aged. I had overestimated the amount of blood there would be in the streets of the world so I never found my way home. Instead I found a woman who loved me and would take my wounded finger in her mouth and suck each drop of blood until her tongue lapped at the cut for more. I think it was all she ate or drank, and when I grew old, the wound slowed to a trickle. Blood only fell from it once or twice a week, and she grew hungry. We went our separate ways.

With only one drop of blood left, I decided to solve my murder. I took up a knife for the first time and cut open the stiff, red envelope that had killed me so long ago. It was an invitation to a birthday party for the gardener who salted the earth where the rose had once grown. It was many years ago.

I have never forgiven him for the rose, but I forgive him for my death which occurred years, months, minutes, seconds before I was intended to draw my last breath of pollen and marshmallows in the poppy field.

Seven

My untimely death comes at the hands of natives. They suffocate me with wonder and love, but I do not die yet. They hold me tighter than I have ever been held before in smallpoxed forearms, and my nose is in one chest, many chests, breathing in antiquities, beads, cornsilk. How were you made this way? I ask. How are you, clay pot? How are you, glass circle?

The natives are bashful. They take pipes from their clay pots and knock out the blood and dust and dirt. The natives say they want to tell me a joke.

Joke.
Deep in America, the one behind the Kum and Go, three men are captured by a tribe of natives.

Not Joke.
At this point they look deep into each other's beads and nod appreciatively.

Joke.

The natives tell the tourists they can choose death or bunga-bunga. The first chooses bunga-bunga.

Not Joke.

The natives are bashful. This might be a little off-color, they say. I tell them I have heard this joke before. Where I'm from it was roo-roo, not bunga-bunga, I say.

The natives are not pleased. What's roo-roo? they ask. They twist their beads and beat their pots. I tell them like this.

Joke.

The one that chooses roo-roo is led into a grass hut.

Not Joke.

I am bashful. I look at the ground and cannot say the words. The natives threaten death or roo-roo if I do not tell them what roo-roo is. I tell them roo-roo is like bunga-bunga, but we have all forgotten so much. They scream and throw corn. They call it maize. I tell them what we call turtles and puppies and remote controls and Kum and Gos. My untimely knowledge comes in handfuls. The natives calm down, blow nut-meggy smoke out their pipes, and sit on their Stain-Master carpet. They ask again in proud voices, but I cannot stop blushing.

Joke.
My untimely death comes at the hands of natives. I go last and choose death. They smile. Death comes at the hands of braves and tribesmen and witch doctors and regular doctors and Lou Diamond Phillips, who smiles widest, as he straps me to the gurney and rubs pungent alcohol on my forearm.

Not Joke.
Where I am there are words I cannot say and stories I cannot tell.

Eight

My untimely death comes from a misstep. My untimely death comes from a footfall. They taught us that land mines are everywhere and so it comes as no surprise when my boot finds one in the parking lot of the mall where I had come to browse racks of clothes, try on new boots, and demo a treadmill which they taught us is the only safe way to walk. My untimely death happens on a cloudy day without wind. I take small pleasure in lighting up the sky and blowing leaves from the fake trees in the parking lot medians.

This was meant to be.

My father died of a land mine in his high school's cafeteria while my mother, safely teenage pregnant, bought a nickel carton of skim milk.

His mother, my unknown grandmother, died when the airplane she was returning home on hit a land mine on a runway and skidded to a fiery stop near Terminal C, where years later, as a boy, I stood watching bottle-nosed planes rocket off while waiting for the funeral of my other grandmother who, like me, took a misstep onto a land mine in a parking lot. She had stopped to ask for directions to a land mine removal service.

We have a term for this: nevermine. No one found this ironical because we have no term for that when it comes to land mines.

Some terms invented to deal with the threat of land mines that did not exist before:

Miniacal—Mad with worry over the threat of land mines.
Misstep-child—One orphaned by land mines.
Church—Place where we are pretty sure there are no land mines.
God?—The answer to the question of who put land mines everywhere.

It's natural that a religion formed around the land mines since we already had satellite television chan-nels and soft drinks and school yard games devoted to them. True believers wear orange jumpsuits and no shoes. They leisurely drag their toes along sand, gravel, cement, or bluegrass as they walk and hold dances, red rover tournaments, and go on long hikes around the country. They have yet to decide whether they are hoping to step on mines or trusting that they will be kept safe from them. First they want to elect a pope and then he will decide.

We have a word for them, too.

I wear boots and a yellow sweater. I skip on the tips of my toes just like everyone who doesn't wear orange. We all skip toward the mall. We look happy.

Nine

My untimely death comes as deletion. It comes with Whiteout. The tiny brush starts at my toes, and as it tickles knees, belly, nipples, I disappear. Whiteout fills my mouth and tastes of fertilizer, Du Pont, and vodka. Whiteout clogs my nostrils, and I go to my death white with fear and whiteout while a crunchy stretch of empty space on the page makes a grave of me.

A blue Bic writes "salt" in the empty space. I am confused. Brushed away by teethy white in my prime, I make lists of sentences to understand how "salt" could have replaced [me].

With more (salt; [me]) this pot roast would be even better.

I like (salt; [me]) more than pepper.

Honey, we're out of (salt; [me]).

It's like rubbing (salt; [me]) in her wound.

Is that (salt; [me]) organic?

But I don't see myself in a sentence with a question mark.

Dead, I try adverbs and gerunds and the whole of grammar to make my sentence. I construct recipes that include a pinch of (salt; [me]) and write songs with words that will rhyme with salt and [me]. The only word I know that rhymes with both is 'cattleman' so I only write country-western songs.

I hear (salt; [me]) left town.

I think I could love (salt; [me]) over time.

Does this have (salt; [me]) in it?

But I don't see myself in a sentence with a question mark.

I've had enough (salt; [me]) for one lifetime.

When I find my sentence I will roll over in my chemical grave and sleep. When I understand how salt and [me] can make meaning I will open my eyes and take a deep breath and lick my lips and white, white, white.

Ten

I go to my untimely death callow and weeping. But it is okay because my untimely death is undertaken by cowards and there are many tears on the ground, not all of which are mine. They make a great puddle. After I die, the cowards cry until the tears are an ocean and they join me in this ignoble passing. I was a coward, too.

But before my death, I crouched beneath the cowardly scythe and spoke devotion to gods I never knew and countries I never saw. Whose hands held it and whose hands didn't, I knew not. My teared vision was a prism and all the faces round me were impeached and exonerated because the cowardly scythe, though sharp, was small, and the hands, though delicate, were large. I was ready this time, but the scythe fell from shaking fingers and the cowards wailed with me on the ground.

Before the scythe, the cowards decided to behead me. One coward, whose name I believe to have been Marvin, happened to have a guillotine. They put me face up instead of face down, and as they locked my neck in the brace I meet each of their eyes. They all looked away, faces grim, committed to my death right up until the moment where they placed their hands on the mortal lever and took them off again. Then they hugged each other as I watched clouds pass overhead.

Things clouds looked like on the day of my death:

An apple.
Myrna Loy.
Clean white underwear.
My childhood beagle.

Before the guillotine, the cowards tricked me into the woods. A coward myself, I shook as I walked by the trunks of trees behind which I saw blinking eyes. A green apple fell at my feet. I picked it up and looked it over, scanning the trees to see where it had come from, but the eyes had disappeared. I threw the apple away and kept on until another green apple hit me in the shoulder. Then another in the stomach. I bent over and saw green apples begin to pile up before me.

Eat one, a voice said. They're not poisoned.

I walked on, already forgetting what they promised me—their great betrayer—would await me in the woods. I only wanted to leave, but more green apples fell in my path. The ground was covered in red leaves and green apples, each one perfectly shaped and polished. The cowards threw and threw until one hit me just so. I fell over onto the apple-covered ground.

I wake up underneath the guillotine. Then, the scythe. Now I do what they fear most. I stand up from the chopping block and pluck an apple off the ground. It is the greenest apple I have ever seen, exactly the color of sour, and as I bite into it the juices run down my chin and hit the earth only a moment before the cowards' first tears.

How did I betray the cowards? I wonder before my eyes close for the final time. This, I realize. This.

Eleven

I am allergic to my untimely death. I die in a fit of sneezes, and I sneeze still. When I think death, when I write death, when I see death, my lungs fill with fluid and hives conquer my skin so that if one of the other dead were to kiss me they might drown, or if they were to touch me they would only grace the bug bite-like Braille rising red from my flesh. These bumps accompany me throughout this heaven. The others stare and whisper when I pass, as if my tortured death is contagious.

I find a blind man—there are still blind people here, though not the people who were blind before—and ask him to read my body to me:

Apple carnival thither bear binder own squishy marsh bear (again) fire Tuesday hear so parker framing bias nevertheless bog swallow heavy hide whiz asunder

Queensbury pastry sought Geoff hallowed Wabasha thyme dolorous incisor foolscap run you whiz (again) donkey want over over (again).

I beg him to tell me more, but the person says there is no time in death for it. At the mention of the word, I take ill for the second final time and die (again).

In this heaven people only speak Spanish. When a blind Spaniard touches the hives on my arm she reads me different words:

Hola, mi nombre es Kevin. ¿Quién es el alcalde?

But my name isn't Kevin, I say.

I die again when the *Nacionale*s start a civil war. I wait it out with Manchego and crackers, never leaving or seeing a twice-dead corpse until Dead Franco takes power and I open my windows to better see the fireworks. The smell of revolution rises from the street. I sweat. I cough, cough, cough. I shock. I cardiac arrest. I pass.

New heaven is for blind people. My hives are worse than ever. I am passed around as great literature. Every blind person in heaven has a turn reading me. Chapter

One is elbow. Chapter Two is calf and so on until every blind person ends with a deep kiss. I win their greatest literary prize. When an old woman finishes with her kiss I ask her what I am about. Like every great story, she says. Love and death. There will be no sequels.

Dead again, my next heaven is only beagle puppies. I bathe in the river. Their judgeless tongues lick me dry. We are all young, and there is no kissing or civil war or blind people here. My hives erase themselves back into my arm, unread.

Twelve

My untimely death is a colorless starvation. My last April on this Earth is snowy and the ground is white and the water is frozen white and at night when white clouds break, white snow stops, I raise white milk with white hand and go white. I put the milk down. I push away the mashed potatoes. My stomach turns when my beautiful baby girl offers me vanilla ice cream.

When the snow melts the grass peeks through the mud. Again I am betrayed by color when I play with my daughter in the park. Green blossoms fall in an easy breeze and my clothes get covered in the green grass. At home my wife offers me spinach salad. I run to the restroom and throw up a stomach full of grass clippings.

My wife, a sweet woman, less beautiful than my daughter, offers me green tea when I open the door. I run back in again.

In June the sun is so yellow that it gives me chills and lemonade gives me fevers. I cut yellow foods out entirely and lose corn, corn dogs, mustard, and Twinkies. I can't go to the state fair.

For an entire week in September I ask my wife to feed me only Swiss chard. There is a day when I eat a can of tomatoes bigger than a toddler. The leaves of the maple tree start to fall like bloody stars and when I see red, I begin to think blood, birth, death, blood, red.

Until October I can eat orange. Every morning I bake myself two pumpkin pies until Halloween when the smell of them concusses me, concusses me so bad I fall back into bed and don't rise until late when I eat a cartons of blueberries. When I kiss my wife goodnight I leave an imprint of purple lips on her cheek. Even my tears turn violet. I ruin towel after towel.

Purple and blue are denied me when I go to the ocean. It is a parking lot of unfathomable magnitude. I tell myself repeatedly that I want to drink every drop. The knowledge that I will never be able to finish it makes the color toxic.

I am left with only the black and the clear. I have my

wife char everything until it is unrecognizable. I get by like this through most of the winter until the nights get long and in my delirium begin to suspect my wife is feeding me charcoal briquettes. This food, whatever it once was, is unimaginably hard at the core but flaky on the outside. I eat it with tongs and dip it into corn syrup and Sprite until, paranoid of diabetes, I begin to sprinkle it with only water. But the nights, the starless, moonless nights.

And so the clear. I live on the clear until those first sick days after the white fades away and the green comes before the red, orange fall and black, black. But I see my wife and daughter on the other side of a glass window. They wave and smile, but behind glass they are so far away that clear becomes disgusting to me. I deny all food and water. Breathing makes me sick. I cannot see my family through the toxic air. I say goodbye without opening my mouth. Finally, having dieted on the opaque and feasted on the translucent, I die full of light.

Thirteen

My untimely death comes at the hands of ex-lovers whom I had imagined still occupied the one-bedroom apartments and three-story houses where they had left me, or I left them, many years ago. But now they've come back for me and they come back with intensity directly proportional to how much I loved them. They have perfect intelligence and know without my ever having told a soul how much I cared about them in the time we were together.

It is not surprising that they knew, and always knew.

The first, someone I knew years ago and loved little, slaps me in the face as soon as I open my door in the morning. Hello, I say, rubbing my cheek. How have you been? You look good.

I get no response or second slap. That comes later when the next one, a person I dated only recently, slaps me twice. Stupidly, not yet understanding what is happening, I say the same thing.

But it is true. Both do look good. They all look good. The one who punches me as I turn around after getting coffee, the one who kicks me over as I bend down to tie my shoe, the one who pushes me in front of traffic as I wait at a cross walk—all of them. And to all of them I say the same thing until it is the ones I really loved. Then I say, Hello. How have you been? You look good. Are you seeing anyone?

This only causes them to kick my ribs or swing the baseball bat or punch my kidneys harder.

There are not as many as I thought there would be. After being scarred in a fire by my prom date, I know I am already up to you and that my time is running out. Still, you don't come back to me quickly. This is so like you, I think. I have lots of time to think while in traction. I wait for you for months, and I begin to worry you aren't coming. Did I not love you as much as I thought? Or was the order really about how much they loved me? Maybe it was a coincidence—or just how it had to be—that the order was the same. Maybe you did not love me at all.

So I rejoice when you come. The hospital is still bright at night, but somehow you slip in through the shadows. Down the hallway people are crying. Things are beeping, respirators exhaling, nurse's feet tapping, yet you come in noiselessly.

Hello, I say, How have you been? You look good. Are you seeing anyone? I miss you.

I add that last part in without meaning to, but it is true. I hope you know that, before you lower the pillow over my face. The beeps, the respirators, the foot tapping all grow faster and faster until it is one great noise.

I know this is all my fault.

Fourteen

My untimely death takes all spring. In the winter I one-up Thoreau and move to the center of Lake Franklin-upon-Burbank to be away from it all, to reconnect with the world as it was meant to be experienced. I thought I would freeze to my untimely death, because I live without shelter and scavenge for food among the ice and snow. The first night I make a pillow of snow and sleep beneath the stars. In my dreams I can see fish looking up at me through the ice.

In the morning I scavenge food at the ranger station. I have more luck. They have a fire hose at the ranger station and as I walk outside I borrow it, like Thoreau might have, and turn the water on, like William James might have. I walk back to my home in the center of the lake. I drag the hose behind me, the water freezing, and as it touches the ice it forms a wall splitting the lake in twain. I never set foot on the north side of the lake again as I find myself stuck behind the wall on the south side.

Though I never again see anyone from the north side of the lake, I imagine them vulgar and blasphemous and pugilistic. Beneath my feet though, I can see fish skirt the new boundary without hesitation and I am as envious as I am suspicious.

Back at my home, I use the hose to build ice walls with ice siding and ice bay windows. The water from the hose never ceases so I continue to build. I make a garage with a work bench and an anvil. I make an atrium with roses. When I try to rest the hose begins to make an unsightly hill so I take it up again and conquer the hill, like Roosevelt might have, and build a memorial on it. It is a memorial to everything, and all winter as I continue to expand my house—glancing over my shoulder to the north so often that in the morning my right cheek is sunburned, in the afternoon, my left—that as my house grows I find new things to memorialize.

On the day I spray a memorial to the sun it reappears again, like Eugene Debs might have, and a yellow plague spreads across the ice. In all directions there is only light, and I am blinded. Still it is cold, and I memorialize my blindness by making more hills, frozen Braille, even though I don't know the language, just big bumps that spell out my plea to God.

But it is only the sun that runs its fingers over them, I know.

I feel water collect at my feet. I go into the guest room and the ice duvet is gone. The iced kangaroo has left and soon the entire ice zoo. In my hand the hose sprays stronger than ever, but I cannot recreate what has melted away from me.

Soon there is no ice, just lake, and north and south are one. I am underwater. I let go the hose. It is at home. I feel fish brush against my fingers. I dream I chase them up, up.

Fifteen

As I always suspected it would, my untimely death comes when my plane crashes into an island. My death does not come in the crash but in waiting out the hunger and sun of the marooned. I knew this was coming yet I flew everywhere. There are those who foresee similar deaths as their silver rocket crumbles against a mountain or an ocean. Or wings fail and they simply tumble to the ground like a penny might. And so they never set foot in a plane. They drive to Grandma's at Easter. They drive to Florida in tan station wagons and take cruises and then drive back home again where they leave the station wagon idling in the garage, a sentry.

They fear planes so they live without them. They live forever. At night they wander the streets looking up to the sky and shaking their fists.

But me, I travel over brown continents and blue oceans. I become rich and buy my own plane. I never land. Mid-air refueling is dangerous, but still we hover over the Earth like a cloud. The pilot teaches me to pilot. He takes the last parachute with him when I ask him to leave. I fly alone.

On the ground the immortals shake fists at me as they refuel their station wagons.

I take to flying with a blindfold and turning off the running lights. I fly upside down for an entire year. I pretend I am a skywriter and write out long letters to my grandma in perfect, invisible cursive:

Dear Grandma,

I hope you didn't miss me at Easter these last five years. It was always my favorite holiday because of the foot smell of boiled vinegar when we dyed the eggs. Did I ever tell you I once drank some of the vinegar? I was maybe six or seven and did it while you and Dad weren't looking. It smelled reassuringly like familiar sweat. It tasted disastrously like familiar sweat.

Toodeloo,

And as I go to sign my name, I dive too low at the nadir of my looping cursive 'J' and crash into an island.

Ambulances come. I send them away because I've grown afraid of cars. Reporters take pictures, tell me it's Nantucket. I tell them an island is an island. This time I write real letters to my grandma about how there is no hope of rescue.

When I take my last breath, I am thinking of a pellet of dye unfurling into hot vinegar and how I read my death in it.